Pam

**The City of Stories**

Happy reading

Lynn Clement

x

# The City of Stories

## Lynn Clement

Chapeltown Books

British Library Cataloguing in Publication Data

A Record of this Publication is available from the British Library

ISBN 978-1-910542-81-1

This edition published 2021 by Chapeltown Books
Manchester, England

# Contents

# Introduction

Welcome to *The City of Stories*.

Lose yourself in these short tales ranging from dark mood accounts of murder and mental illness to hilarious observations on pelvic thrusts in later life.

Read about Jacko and his struggles to make sense of his three-year-old world, and Freddie, Gretchen, and Tom on their new learning journey.

Peer into the future with *The Tree Museum,* or step beyond this earthly realm altogether.

Cosy up with a cuppa to reminisce on your childhood and then be made to think of other children and their lot in life. Or try a glass of *Malbec*, as you read *The Window,* you might need it!

Be prepared to experience a rollercoaster of emotions as you engage with all the different characters and find out how they solve their problems. Whether it's The Beginner's Sumo Wrestling classes for the over-seventies, wing-walking in *Tena Pants,* or trying to escape an oppressive regime before you are eliminated, read how our heroes cope with all that life throws at them.

After reading *The Guest House*, you will always check your mobile battery life.

Do you notice the homeless? Read *I Was You Once* and maybe you will look again!

And just what is Millicent's secret in *A Woman's Place?*

I thoroughly enjoyed writing and compiling this book of short stories, flash fiction, and poems. Life is different for every one of us. My stories are reflections of some of the things I have observed in my short time on this earth, and even some projections for the future!

So, settle down with your drink of choice and I hope you enjoy reading *The City of Stories.*

# Word Police

Thoughts ought to out themselves.
But now and again they remain
hidden,
locked in a pocket of self-doubt,
where silence gives licence to grow
and, sometimes they clash as they bash around the walls of my brain,
trying to escape the rain, capable of keeping them contained.
But, when a blank page makes eye contact, a burning desire begins,
Igniting the damp that hampers, creating a head of steam,
clouds that billow and flow
                    spill over the rim and plop
                              onto the open book
                                        that when I look,

is filled with words,
which have emerged from deep within the confines that,
from time to time I need to police,
and ensure they're released – to be free.

# A Woman's Place

'Time to borrow the ox,' said Wyatt to his wife Millicent. 'I'm going to Audley's and will fetch it back anon.'

'Aye.'

'I'll want hot flummery when I get back,' Wyatt barked. 'And you make sure you pray for good weather whilst I be gone.'

'Aye,' was the reply.

For the past three years, Millicent hadn't prayed for the weather. Yet the crop had yielded well. But that was her secret.

Millicent went to the barn. This was her walk every time Wyatt went away. There were no children, so she was alone. Well… not quite.

Once, whilst Wyatt was at Audley's Strip, she'd heard a noise coming from the barn. It was like no other she had ever heard. Heading there she was suddenly bowled over by a blinding flash. She picked herself up from the muck and cagily opened the door. Shielding her eyes from the brightness of what appeared to be a woman's body ablaze on the wooden wall, Millicent could hardly breathe. She held her chest in pain.

The woman on the wall spoke. 'Today in rural Winchester the weather will be cold. Over the next few days there will be sunshine and rain, perfect spring growing weather.'

'Thank you, Lucy,' said another voice and the picture faded.

Millicent, panting, had slumped against the barn wall.

Each time Wyatt went away the *shiny-woman* would appear. Millicent coyly began to suggest to Wyatt when to travel and fetch the Ploughing-Ox, so that the crop would grow well in the weather. He was reluctant to accept her advice, she being a woman, but believing Millicent had great powers of prayer, he did so. After all, for the past few years they had been well fed.

This time when Millicent entered the glowing barn, the *shiny-woman* wasn't there, but a gaggle of women instead.

The flaxen-haired one said, 'So, on *Loose Women* today, we discuss marital relations and a woman's place in the home.'

Millicent settled down in the straw to listen.

# Cleanliness is Next to Godliness

'Where's Mum?' asked Ray Boswell.

'In the bathroom,' replied his eldest.

'Right, we're going,' Ray slammed the door to make his point.

In their newly refurbished bathroom, Samantha was washing her hands.

A sticky note was on the kitchen cupboard door above the kettle, where Ray knew Samantha would see it. *Don't forget your doctor's appointment!* When she saw it, she lifted the note from the door and walked to the bin. Hitting the pedal, she dropped the note in, and then wiped her feet on the mat just inside the kitchen door. She went to the sink. The teeth of the nail brush snarled at her, as she picked it up and began scrubbing at the tips of her fingers. The red water swirled down the plughole.

The clock chimed ten. She should have set off by now if she were to be on time. Samantha finished applying the plasters and put her gloves on. Lifting her raincoat from the stand she carefully manoeuvred her arms into the sleeves, leaving the buttons undone despite the biting cold that would hit her outside. The belt hung loose and banged on her leg as she walked.

Samantha crossed the road, avoiding the urine-soaked bus stop and quickened her pace. A film of sweat formed on her top lip and she felt sick. Fishing in her pocket she brought out today's freshly laundered handkerchief and dabbed at her skin. She felt the familiar burning sensation in her throat and tried to swallow it down but vomited on the pavement.

She had to make this appointment. Ray was at the end of his tether with her. She needed help.

Samantha pushed open the wooden door, looking immediately for the lavatory.

'Welcome,' said a deep voice.

She went in.

'How can I help you?' he said.

'Forgive me, Father, for I have sinned,' said Samantha.

'Tell me, my child,' said the priest.

Samantha followed him into the confessional.

# Serendipity

Joe knocked on the shabby looking red door. He wasn't sure what had possessed him to follow the woman. He was going to be late for work now. She was a quick walker and by the time he'd made his mind up to return the shoe, she'd dashed off. Luckily, he'd kept her in sight whilst fighting the early morning rush crush and now here he was outside her door.

'Yes,' she said on opening the door.

*Not a warm welcome*, thought Joe.

'I – err… you dropped your shoe, that is, your baby dropped the shoe.' Joe was never the most articulate.

'Oh, thanks,' she said, taking the tiny blue shoe from Joe's hand. The door was closing when Joe decided to put his foot in it.

'Hey,' said the woman with the golden curls, tied up in a purple scarf.

'I'm sorry,' explained Joe, 'I can hear your baby crying.'

'That's none of your business,' snapped the woman.

'It's such a high-pitched cry,' said Joe.

'Is it really?' asked the woman sarcastically. 'I hadn't noticed all these days and nights.'

Joe saw her dark green eyes harden.

Her pretty face became weary. 'Jog on, mister,' she said and tried to close the door again.

Joe put his hand on the handle now, 'I need to come in,' he insisted. The smell of stale milk and dirty nappies drifted up the grimy uncarpeted corridor. The baby's cry was persistent and uncomfortable. 'I only want to look at the baby.'

'What are you, some kind of perv? Get lost, mister.'

Joe pushed the door and followed the wail to a tiny bedroom, where the baby lay in a crib, lovingly decorated with hand embroidered bumpers and a purple patchwork quilt. He bent over the cot and lifted the baby, confirming his suspicion.

He thumbed his mobile. 'My name is Doctor Joseph Kent, send an ambulance to 6 Meade Terrace and quickly, this baby has meningitis.'

The baby's mother slumped to the floor.

Joe sat beside her and cradled the baby in the crook of his arm. He held the woman's hand as they waited for the ambulance.

# Donna

*Don't jump,* were the words that usually woke Donna up; sometimes with a scream, other times with a leap from the bed.

This time Jim's arm had pinned her down, not wanting a repeat of the cut on her forehead, where Donna had bashed it on the wardrobe when her foot had caught in the bedsheets the last time, she'd had her recurring nightmare.

'I'm okay,' she said sitting upright.

Jim rolled over.

Donna tucked the sheets around her neck like a baby in its cradle – swaddled. She lay staring at the shadows creeping over the ceiling. At the slam of a car door, she edged further down the bed. Jim was breathing rhythmically again. It was about three hours before the birds would sing Donna back to sleep, so she counted. She always counted now: steps to the bathroom, steps to the front door, steps down the path – when she *could* get beyond the front door.

She heard the bass thump of her neighbour Eddie's car as he returned from a night out. Donna counted how many seconds it took for Eddie to ping the car door lock, tramp the gravel path, and shut his front door. Fifteen seconds.

The distant traffic noise had become less frequent. Donna guessed it was about 3 am. She used to enjoy the soft swoosh on the A-road as the cars passed the house. It was soporific – before. The clatter of train wheels caught on the wind and Donna counted – ten seconds.

Jim was snoring. The bedside clock was ticking.

Donna felt cold. She looked at Jim and turned on her side to face the wardrobe, being careful not to rouse him. Lying there motionless, her eyes filled, and tears spilled onto her cheeks. She'd learnt to do this silently. The face in the wardrobe mirror stared at her, mocking her weakness. Donna counted as the salt worked its way into the corners of her mouth.

A low growl began outside the window. A tom cat was toying with its prey. Overpowering it, he dragged it onto the driveway. The guttural sound she heard next was a sign of his satisfaction. Donna's knees drew up to her chest and she wrapped her arms around them. She closed her eyes. It took forty seconds to stop.

The morning sun peeped over the yellow kitchen café-curtains. On the solid pine table, tea was steaming; chocolate biscuits were arranged in a line on the plain white plate. Donna held the crumpled paper tightly in her fist.

In the next room the counsellor was talking to Jim.

'Yes, it was a bad night. Two screams and almost a leap out of bed again,' he said.

'It will take time, Jim. I do think Donna is responding.'

'I'm not sure,' said Jim. 'She's not even attempted to get out of the house this week.'

'No? The court's letter won't have helped,' replied the counsellor.

Donna was counting her steps to the front door from the kitchen –

twenty steps. Twenty steps that began a nightmare. She fingered the door chain and pushed down hard on the handle, it held firm. She counted twenty steps back to the kitchen table.

The chicken for dinner was now in her eye-line. Its legs were trussed with ties. The exposed goose-pimpled breasts made her retch. She kicked the pedal and knocked the insinuation into the bin. She banged her fist down hard on the lid.

'Donna, are you ready to have a chat now?' asked her counsellor settling down opposite her at the kitchen table.

Donna's eyes closed and opened again, after she'd taken a deep breath to the count of ten. She tried to smile but couldn't force the corners of her mouth upwards.

The counsellor, over the rim of her teacup, tried to look into Donna's eyes. Donna was looking at the tablecloth.

Jim had opened his newspaper to the inside page where he knew it was hidden. He already had the information that was now being made public. Monday, January 15th was the date of the trial at Winchester Crown Court. Almost exactly one year to the day, 352 days to be precise; 8448 hours, over 500,000 minutes since his wife opened the door and in seconds their lives had been changed for ever.

In the kitchen Donna had drunk her tea and rearranged the chocolate biscuits.

The counsellor noted that Donna had held eye contact with her for approximately five seconds. The counsellor considered this to be an improvement. She moved her open palm to the middle of the table.

Donna's eyes closed once more but she put her hand in the counsellor's.

The counsellor's fingers closed around Donna's. They sat there in silence for as long as Donna needed to count.

# New Leaf

'I'm turning over a new leaf,' I say to my mother.

She looks at me with sadness in her eyes.

'No, I mean it, Mum, this time it's for real.'

She kisses my cheek and waves as she gets to the door.

Flopping back on my pillow, I am exhausted at the pretence of it all. Closing my eyes, the old pictures come. I was in a pink frilly frock, or was it purple – lilac maybe? We were in the back entry to our two-up two-down in the heart of Salford. Five years old and happy as Larry, whoever he is? Why do people say that, happy as Larry? It's a good name though, short for Laurence. Nearly as good as the one I picked.

Another memory flashes in my mind, that one where I was with my cousins, Kathleen, and Frank. We were playing by the River Irwell. Frank was showing off as usual. I adored him. He was my hero in a way, and I wanted to be like him. After that day, I wanted to be him.

We were mucking around at the water's edge and the dog fell in. I didn't know any of us knew how to swim. We didn't have lessons and I don't remember our parents taking us swimming either. But Frank loved that dog, and he wasn't about to let him drown. Frank dived in; well belly-flopped really with an almighty splash that sent the water splattering over me and Kathleen. He was a big lad, Frank, and he was strong. He got the dog, Laddie, to the side where he could scramble out.

Me and Kathleen managed to drag Frank halfway up the bank where he was able to grab some roots and pull himself onto the grass. He lay there flat on his back, panting, a bit like the dog had. Laddie recovered quickly and was now licking his privates.

I remember laughing out loud. Breaking the tension, I said, 'Don't you do that, Frank!' I think Frank swore at me, but in that moment, I fell in love.

The love wasn't for Frank as such, although I liked him a lot; he was my cousin after all, but for what he was. I hadn't dived in. Kathleen hadn't dived in, but Frank had. Was that when I realised, I was wrong? Something was wrong. I'm not sure really. It's taken me forty years to know.

The nurse interrupts my thoughts. 'Hello, Frankie,' she says. 'How are you feeling today?' She reaches for the medication as she speaks.

'I'm okay,' I say. 'Just had a visit from Mother.'

'How's she taking it?'

'The usual,' I say, 'trying to put a brave face on it.'

'It's a big thing for her,' says Nurse Downing.

'It's a big thing for me,' I say.

She tells me the surgeon will be here in a little while and gives me my pre-op medicine. I'm hoping it will calm the nerves. I am so scared but now I know I need this. This is my new leaf. No more depression. No more suicide attempts. No more longing to be someone that my body says I'm not. The real me revealed.

I begin to drift off and I can see my mother's sad eyes saying goodbye to her little girl at the ward door.

# The Phone Rang Twice

The phone rang for a second time, but I still didn't get up. I'd left it in the kitchen after I'd dropped the pan of boiling potatoes all over the floor. My hand hurt even after running it under the cold tap and my toes looked like those pink shrimps from *Iceland* that my mother used to buy for Christmas Day.

I'd had my cry and a scream but now I was drained, unlike the potatoes that hadn't even made the colander. Yet one more incident, one more accident, one more rubbish thing that's happened lately. I'm done.

No, phone, I am not going to answer you, and get a load of verbal about why I haven't made it into work again or paid the car tax or made my doctor's appointment or... You can stay there and ring to your heart's content. It's funny how we still say 'ring' even though most phones have totally different tones to a ring. Mine barks.

Billy was so lovely. I adored that pooch with his floppy little ears and twitchy nose and the way he looked at me as if he understood everything I said. Another bark – someone is persistent.

'Get lost, whoever you are!'

I look at the orange curtains, glowing like a furnace with the sunlight trying to get through. It's stifling. I've not drawn them together well enough, as a small slice of light is playing on my glass coffee table. I push my iPad into the gap and the light dulls.

My eyes are tired. It would be so easy to close them and go. I might see Billy. Do I believe in all that? I don't know. I don't believe in anything much anymore. It's too hard to keep trying.

My stomach gurgles the way a sink does when it's emptying. I'm empty, yet my head weighs so much. I curl my legs up on the chair and lay my heavy head down on the arm. It's not soft and my ear hurts.

A ping wakes me. I'm not moving; I know it's the iPad. It'll only be one more nasty comment. I don't know why it chooses to let me know that someone else thinks I'm a bitch or a cow or an ugly f***ing dog murderer.

Why are they called trolls? Big feet? Little bodies? Or something else?

The phone barks again. Closing my eyes, I see Billy under the wheels of the car. I'll never drive it again. I'm sorry I reversed over him. I didn't mean to hurt him; he was my neighbour. I kind of loved him. Grief does funny things to people. My mother always said it can send some a bit loopy. My neighbours are loopy. Loopy with grief for Billy. So loopy they've turned into trolls.

One more bark and then it stops. I keep my eyes closed and wait for the dark.

# The Last Train

The thick smoke is spreading and beginning to envelope the carriages. Standing here on the side of the hill I can see it all perfectly. It's like a scene from a black and white movie, only slowed down. Why are they all so slow? Maybe it's one of those emergency disaster practices.

A scream from a stretcher tells me it's no practice; either that or there is some serious overacting going on.

I can smell it now, kind of like a huge dodgy electrical wire. My mouth tastes like I have been chewing rusty nails and it makes me gag.

Another body is carried on a stretcher. I can't tell if it's a man or a woman. A white mask covers its face; at least it's not *the blanket* yet. A gust of wind catches the smoke and throws it towards me, so I move further up the hill.

I can hear a mobile phone ringing in one of the black zipped up bags below me, and it sparks a memory.

'Yes, Mother,' I'd said. 'I made the 7.30. I'll get there on time. You worry too much, but hey thanks for waking me.' I'd hung up.

I remember – people were talking into the air, headphones buzzing, newspapers rustling, laptops open, the smell of coffee, then... metal grinding, windows rattling, lights flashing, shouting, screeching; a bang – sending objects flying where they'd no right to be flying, a faint rumble raced into a roar, accompanied by the stench of... burning hog roast, choking fumes, spitting coughs, and sobbing; then – silence.

That wind is really annoying me now, sending the smoke swirling around me. I try to waft it away, but it won't go.

I want to phone my mum but haven't got my mobile; I must have dropped it in the panic. Looking down to the bottom of the hill, I count eight black bags and another one is being added.

There's somebody coming up the hill. It's the guy in the grey suit with the slicked back hair. He sits opposite me every day and does his *Time*s crossword, whilst sipping de-caf coffee from the trolley service.

'You okay, mate?' He stops. It's clearly a stupid question as he doesn't answer.

The phone in the black bag rings again; it's playing *Sweet Child of Mine*. It's someone's mother.

That blasted smoke is all around me now. I flap at it but can't even see the hand in front of my face.

Someone taps me on my shoulder, and I turn round. I can just about make out a queue in front of me. What are they queuing for? I count them, there are seven. I don't want to be number eight, so I turn again – but the man in the grey suit waves me forward. I shout at him to go back down, but he just keeps coming.

The smoke is black and dense, and I want to cry. I need to speak to my mum. Number nine points to the top of the hill. Number seven looks over her shoulder and beckons me with encouragement. The smoke ahead is lifting, and I can see her eyes. They're kind and remind me of my mother. The phone in the black bag rings again.

Looking at the brow of the hill, I can see it's green and dappled with small yellow flowers, no smoke, just fluffy white clouds; it looks quite inviting. I try to smile at number seven, and she smiles back. I turn to the man in the grey suit, who nods in the direction of the clouds, and I realise it's time to go.

Falling in line with the others, I leave the clutches of the black vapour and slowly make my way towards the grass-topped crest of the hill.

# Freefall

'I've wet myself,' I shouted to Stan Borden.

'Don't worry, the wind will dry it before we arrive,' he replied.

'I've got my *Tena Pants* on anyway.'

'Good news,' he said.

On ten we jumped.

*Waa – what the hell am I doing?* I thought, as I rushed through the cold air.

*You okay?* gestured Stan, forming a circle with his thumb and forefinger and waving it in front of my face.

I nodded.

We were in freefall. I closed my eyes, but that made me feel sick and disorientated, so I opened them again. I saw Stan's arms moving up and down. I thought he was attempting to fly off somewhere, taking me as a piece of carrion. Then it dawned on me, he was trying to untangle the cords.

'Keep still!' he shouted.

Keep still? I wanted to run away as fast as my legs would carry me, but of course, point one: I can't fly, and point two: I was strapped to Stan.

My mind whirred. *It's been a good life,* I thought, *but I wish I'd made up with Dolly before I jumped.*

'Don't be ridiculous,' Dolly had said. 'People don't sky-dive at our age.'

Dorothy is my ever so cautious twin. I always call her Dolly. She doesn't like it much. She enjoys the formality of Dorothy. I think it makes her feel important. She's always been yin to my yang. We married on the same day; her in white, me in red, had our children on the same day, one girl and one boy and always assumed we might even die on the same day. And it looked like this was that day.

I felt a sharp tug under my arms as the parachute opened.

Stan gave me the thumbs up and I reciprocated.

*That was close,* I thought. *Hopefully, Dolly will be okay too.*

I decided to make up with her as soon as I was down. No more parachute jumps for me.

I wonder what she'll think about wing-walking.

# Independence Day

'I do it, I do it,' said Freddie with an excited squeal. He was referring to his buttons that Gretchen had started to fasten.

She smiled down at him, said 'Okay,' and watched patiently. Gretchen had worked hard with Freddie on this lost skill. She'd bought him those threading buttons for kids to play with, to help him improve his manipulation.

He looked up at her and she nodded encouragingly. His bent fingers fumbled over the cardigan buttons. They seemed too tiny for his large hands.

Gretchen's fingers twitched, aching to help him but she knew this was the wrong thing to do. He had to learn. Gretchen smiled every time he sought her approval.

Freddie took five minutes to do his first three buttons. He banged one frustrated hand down on the arm of the chair and laid his chin on his chest.

Gretchen knew from experience this was the time to step in. When he became frustrated, he became tired and disillusioned and that could make for a tricky day. She placed her fingers under his chin and lifted it slightly.

'It's okay, let me help.' she finished the last two buttons. She tucked his treasured Manchester United scarf fringes into his coat and fetched the red stripy throw from the sofa, packing it around him. 'It's cold today.'

At last, they were ready for their weekly trip to the library. They both enjoyed it. Gretchen loved reading stories to Freddie. He always giggled at the funny ones like *The Cat in the Hat* and *Green Eggs and Ham*. These were the books she'd chosen to teach him to read again.

Gretchen had carried out some research into early reading and recognised familiarity was helpful. Freddie loved the repetition and got the rhyme. She'd read the lines and leave the rhyme off at the end and Freddie would complete it. He enjoyed the part in *The Cat in the Hat* where the children say, 'sit, sit, sit' and then he would finish it off when Gretchen said, 'We don't like it one…' with 'bit.' He understood about that.

Freddie's favourite books were about football. He always chose a football book to take home, often the same familiar one, with his heroes, Georgie Best and Denis Law, on the cover.

She pushed him onto the street, sighing as she saw the cars once again parked on the kerb. This was her pet hate. People were so inconsiderate.

'Car,' pointed out Freddie, as Gretchen waited to pass a silver BMW that was parked completely on the pavement.

A motorbike whizzed past them on the cobbled road. Looking over her right shoulder Gretchen manoeuvred Freddie's chair around the silver car.

'Errrr,' said Freddie in time to the wheels bumping over the cobbles.

Gretchen could hear another car approaching behind her so she tried to steer the chair back onto the pavement as quickly as she could. The car behind slowed down and waited for Gretchen to shove Freddie out of harm's way. She acknowledged the driver by giving him a wave. He tooted in appreciation.

'Toot toot,' said Freddie.

'Yes, a car horn,' she said.

Freddie's speech was really coming on now and she took every opportunity to enhance it. They'd worked so hard on vocabulary. She liked to sing to him, and cajoled him to join in. Friday mornings were their karaoke times. Gretchen would put on a CD whilst she did the housework and sang to the familiar songs. When Frank Sinatra sang, she'd hand the furniture-polish bottle to Freddie and he would pretend he was singing along into a mic. He'd mastered *New York, New York* as a phrase and she kept working on the repetition.

It was almost a mile to the library, and it wasn't long before Freddie began drifting off to sleep so Gretchen let her mind shift to Tom. She was looking forward to seeing him again. They always met in the burger bar after visiting the library, where Tom would have a vanilla shake waiting for Freddie and a latte for her.

She touched her hair and flicked the straggles from out of her shirt collar. She wished she'd had time to tie it up in a ribbon. She'd bought some pretty pink ones from Boots last time she'd ventured into town. She felt in her bag – good, her new rose lipstick and the compact mirror were in there. She'd apply the lipstick before they left the library.

Gretchen regretted popping into the supermarket before the library. Friday afternoon was not the best time to push Freddie round the crowds. The tannoy announcer was urgently plugging the latest offers and bargains. Gretchen sighed. She'd been sucked into buying bargains before which often weren't the bargains they were hyped up to be. She only wanted a pierce and ping for her dinner, but not the aromatic Thai curry with a twist that was announced with a flourish. A wandering trolley was blocking the aisle, whilst its elderly owner peered at the prices of minced beef.

'Excuse me,' Gretchen said.

With no hint of apology, he moved his trolley, only for it to drift back into the middle of the aisle once Gretchen and Freddie had passed. The smell of chicken on a rotisserie floated under Gretchen's nose making her mouth water.

'Mmm... smell that chicken. No point getting it though. Only me at home, so a whole chicken would be a waste,' she said to Freddie, who was still dozing. Selecting carbonara pasta that took three and a half minutes to cook, she headed for the checkout. 'Why do they make these aisles so narrow?'

Her *patienceometer* was running low. She'd not had any lunch today, so her blood sugar was probably down. Gretchen grabbed two bags of sweets from the shelves next to the till. Freddie looked like he was still asleep, he could have his later.

In the library, Freddie was a bit grumpy after his nap so there wasn't much reading to be done. Even the librarian's cheery 'afternoon Freddie' didn't change his mood.

Gretchen wondered if he was sickening for something. She felt his forehead; it did feel a bit clammy.

Freddie selected his football book and they headed for the lift.

*Maybe I am pushing him too hard,* she thought. *Maybe I am pushing myself too hard.* She had a headache. Closing her eyes helped. *Perhaps I need to go to the opticians. I'll have a look at my diary and book something.*

When she opened her eyes, Freddie was staring at her. She smiled and he smiled back. Finding the pink lipstick in her bag she applied it carefully, all the while Freddie was staring at her.

'Pretty,' he said.

She smiled again. 'Right, let's go and find Tom.' They headed towards the lift. Gretchen read the sign – *Out of Order.* She sighed.

Freddie began to wail. Heads popped up from books; like that game where you must hit plastic people with a hammer to keep them down.

Gretchen wanted to do just that – bop them down. She felt her cheeks burn and tried to soothe him.

A librarian scurried over to them.

Gretchen held her hands out. 'Well?'

'I'll take you to the staff lift,' said the librarian.

Freddie continued to wail all the way through the Mechanics section and past the Railway shelves. When he saw the Sport books, he stopped wailing.

'More books?' he said.

Gretchen looked at her watch. She put her head down and quickly followed the librarian.

The lift was not fit for purpose and it took careful manoeuvring to get

Freddie in. She let him press the ground floor button, which impressed him. The lift slowly clunked to a halt. Backing Freddie and herself out of it was a feat, as the area in front of the doors was loaded with brown boxes. She clattered into one or two and hoped they were only full of books. A thoughtful mother with twin daughters on either side of her, held the library door open for them.

'Thank you,' Gretchen said.

One of the twins offered Freddie a lick of her lollipop, but he declined.

Blowing slowly through her lips, Gretchen swung him towards the smell of chargrilled meat clinging to the thick air inside the shopping centre. She knew she was running late now and hoped Tom would be there.

Gretchen was pleased to see Tom's huge smile as she strode into the burger bar. She flushed.

Freddie seemed to perk up. He gave Tom his lopsided grin when he saw the milk shake.

'How was your day?' Tom asked.

'Oh eventful,' Gretchen replied.

She began to undo Freddie's buttons.

'I do it,' said Freddie.

'Whoops! Sorry,' she said, giving him her encouraging grin. She inclined her head towards Freddie, showing Tom that Freddie was mastering his doing-up skills.

'Cool,' said Tom.

Tom stroked Freddie's hair and bent down to his eye level.

'Hi, Dad, how are you today? You had a good time with Gretchen?'

Freddie was not able to respond to that level of questioning yet, so he just smiled with one side of his mouth. It had been two years since he'd had his stroke. It came out of the blue. One minute he was a fitness fanatic, jogging in the park, playing football, and running his own business, and the next minute he'd regressed.

Gretchen was a godsend. She gave Tom every Friday off to do some shopping and have some independence from his role as Freddie's sole carer.

As Tom gave Gretchen her coffee his fingers touched hers. She was glad she'd taken the time to paint her nails coral pink today.

'So, did you buy anything?' Gretchen asked lifting the steaming mug to her mouth.

Tom picked up his *House of Fraser* bag. 'Yep, a shirt, want to see?'

'Of course,' she said.

Tom held a pink and purple striped affair up against his chin.

Gretchen giggled.

'Oh, you don't like it?'

'Well, it doesn't exactly go with your lovely red hair.'

'No, perhaps you're right,' said Tom. 'That's the problem with not having anyone with me when I'm shopping.'

'You could take it back next Friday,' said Gretchen.

'Yes,' he said. He sipped his drink. Over the top of his mug Tom looked into Gretchen's dark green eyes. 'Maybe you and Dad could come with me?'

Gretchen blushed again. 'Sure. We could do that, eh, Freddie?'

Freddie sucked on his straw.

Tom sat back in his chair.

'Freddie chose the Georgie Best book again,' said Gretchen.

'Yeah, he was his hero,' replied Tom. 'Heroes come in all sorts of shapes and sizes,' he added. 'Isn't that right, Dad?'

Freddie put down his milk shake, looked at Tom and, catching his eye, winked at him. This time it was Tom's cheeks that turned red. Freddie giggled.

'What are you two up to?' asked Gretchen, detecting some kind of conspiracy.

Tom quickly changed the subject. 'Hey, Dad, I nearly forgot, look what I got you.' He lifted a box onto the table and started to take the lid off.

'I do it, I do it,' said Freddie. He managed to remove the lid and clapped his best working hand against the other hand with joy, at the sight of his new football boots. He tilted the box up to show Gretchen.

She gave Freddie the thumbs up and mouthed, 'wow' at him.

'That's me and you sorted then, Dad – a game of wheelchair footie in the garden later and we'll have cups of *Bovril*.' Smiling at Gretchen he said, 'Don't suppose you fancy coming along – top supporter?'

'Oh well, I err… just bought my pierce and ping dinner,' replied Gretchen, knowing how pathetic she sounded.

'Well, if *Bovril* doesn't tempt you, I have roast chicken from the supermarket we could share after the game.'

'Mmm... chicken,' said Freddie, licking his lips.

Tom and Gretchen laughed out loud. Several customers looked towards them.

'I'll bring my United scarf,' smiled Gretchen.

# Seeing the Light

Della James tried to open her eyes. It was hard; she was groggy. She heard whirring and clanking in the room. She was afraid. There was a pain in the back of her head; it felt like she had been coshed.

She lay still, wondering what she should do. There was a lot of movement around her. One of them touched her arm, but she didn't move a muscle. She could taste the salt on her top lip. More clanking and whirring. Her heart pounded. She wanted to move her hands, remove the blindfold, and find out what they looked like. One of them touched her again, she felt their hot breath on her face, and she recoiled.

Della always thought she was not a racist, but she didn't approve of her country being overrun with foreigners.

*It will all end in tears;* she'd say when her daughter chided her for objecting to Britain's immigration policy. *You mark my words, they'll take all our houses and jobs,* she used to say.

She'd say so in the supermarket and the café and the shop queue, if needed. She was polite but always stuck to her guns. There was a time her daughter didn't talk to her. Della wondered what she would be thinking now. She stiffened as she heard the sound of scissors being tested, opening, and closing near her ears. Her mouth was dry, her palms were wet. The blindfold fell away from her head.

In his clipped English accent acquired at Cambridge University, Rakesh Sharma said, 'Okay, Mrs James, open your eyes please, slowly at first.'

Della did as she was instructed.

'Can you see the light, Mrs James?'

She smiled. 'Yes, I can.'

As Della fully opened her cataract-free eyes she saw his warm brown eyes, framed between a thatch of jet-black hair and a surgical mask.

'You are happy to have come to India for surgery?' he said.

'Oh yes, Doctor,' replied Della.

Della was looking forward to getting back to England. She would call in on her daughter and tell her about the operation. Della could imagine the look on her face. She would definitely do that, but not before she'd seen a bit of India. She'd heard it was lovely.

# Inheritance

Charlie eyed up Emily. She was eating her lunch, the usual mush. She washed it down with lukewarm tea. She wasn't a bad looker for her age. Salt and pepper hair and fairly plump lips for a seventy-year-old. She always wore nice jewellery, which she liked to match with the colour of her cardigans – greens and turquoise today, with emeralds and sapphires. Charlie's eyes twinkled; she was just right.

Bob was also eyeing up Emily. He was eyeing up Charlie too. He peered over the top of his cup, as he raised the sweet tea to his mouth. His lips curled at the thought of Charlie and Emily together. There was just something about Charlie that wasn't quite right. He was a bit young for the home. Sixty-five was young nowadays. Why was he here? Bob had been watching Charlie since he arrived at *Sunny Days Home for the Retired*.

In the lounge after dinner that evening, Charlie bumped into Emily as he headed towards the piano. He gushed an apology and offered to play her a tune on the, 'old Joanna' as he called it.

Bob winced. Emily lapped it up. She joined Charlie in a rendition of *Moon River*. Bob watched.

Within six months there had been two deaths at *Sunny Days,* old Joe Matlock and Jean Corrigan, Emily's best friend and only surviving relative. Jean's funeral was today.

Emily decided to dress up her black sheath-dress with her mother's pearls, handed down to her from her own mother many years ago. She looked in the mirror as she applied a coral lipstick. The tap on the door indicated Charlie was outside, waiting to escort her to the funeral car. She folded the read and re-read solicitor's letter and placed it in her dressing table drawer.

That night after the funeral, Emily didn't notice the drawer was slightly open.

A wedding was the next big event Emily attended – her own. Diamonds were the jewels of the day, earrings set in 18 carat gold, given to her by her new husband. Her romance had been a bit of a whirlwind. She'd had nothing but good luck since she'd had the solicitor's letter, telling her she was the sole survivor of the tontine, secured by her father and his brother, Jean's father. The tontine was now worth £100,000.

There was clinking on a wine glass, as Charlie called all the guests to order. He proposed a toast to the bride and her new husband.

Bob smirked as he raised his wine glass. He smiled at his wife. He fingered the syringe in his pocket. No one had questioned Jean's heart attack, and old Joe Matlock was good practice. Charlie had proved to be a bit of a pushover really. Everyone has their price. A £100,000 inheritance would be very nice indeed.

*And if Charlie thinks he is getting his hush money, he can think again.*

# Carol

'Bye, Carol, I'm off now, see you tomorrow.'

The door clicked shut.

'Uh oh, rumbly tumbly,' Carol said. She opened the fridge door. No lunch. She closed it and it beeped at her, and then began to whirl around. Carol stared. She opened it again. 'No magic food?' Her tummy gurgled.

Carol's slippered feet shuffled to the drawer. She was sure there would be food in the drawer. 'I know Mother has been stockpiling arrowroot biscuits and *Camp* coffee.'

Her brow furrowed. 'New coffee in blue bottles? Mmm... purple blocks – chocolate.' Her stiff fingers eventually peeled back the packaging and she bit into one of the blocks. 'Yuck! It's off.' She spat it into the sink and washed it away. The water made the chocolate foam in the basin.

'Hello,' she said to the cat, who had sauntered into the kitchen. 'I see you've got food.' The cat purred.

Carol eyed the jellied meat; her mouth watered. Her knees creaked and she stroked the cat. His food looked juicy and flavoursome. 'Has Mother given you the tinned steak, puss? We must be short of cash if she's got tinned steak in; we only have that for Sunday when Papa has been drinking again. Why have you got it?'

Carol reached for a spoon from the kitchen side, then pressing her back to the wall she held onto the towel rail and slid down next to the cat. She could smell the stress of those Sunday lunches. She winced and closed her eyes. When she opened them again the kitchen light had gone off, but Carol thought someone was shining a torch beam through the window. She rubbed her cold arms and moved her head from side to side to ease her stiff neck. Blinking her sticky eyelids, she looked ahead and saw a note on one of the doors.

*Carol, your lunch is in here.*
    *Love from Trina x*

Carol looked at puss curled up on her lap. 'Now, why would Trina put my lunch in the washing machine?' she asked him.

# The Morsborough Journey

The road towards Morsborough was dry and dusty, like the back of a slave's throat after picking cotton all day. The sun had fallen from its perch and the night was fighting to get up there, changing the broad-sailed trees into haunting silhouettes.

'I'm sure this is the way,' said Ma to the back of Cody's head.

'Sure as eggs is eggs,' said Lily-May. 'Like she always is.'

'Except this time, she ain't right,' sneered Jake-Wayne. He folded his arms across his fat stomach and huffed. The baby started to wail.

'Shut that hollerin' child up,' Cody yelled at his wife, Louanna.

Louanna took her kerchief from her head and gave it to the baby to suck.

'I'm guessing he's hungry,' stated Ma.

Cody turned the car headlamps on so he could see the bends in the winding road.

'I saw a sign saying Morsborough twenty miles back there,' said Jake-Wayne, hooking his thumb behind his head.

'You can't read, Jake-Wayne, you word blind and ain't that the truth,' Lily-May spat.

Jake-Wayne reached over Ma's lap and pinched Lily-May right on the thigh.

Ma looked at Lily-May wondering what she would do next, but she did nothing.

There was gravel on the road that made the ride bumpy. It was a rock fall from the hills that sandwiched it. Last night there had been some rare rain that had slicked the stones and slid them onto their path.

Cody cursed.

Louanna, looked at him and then at the baby who was now asleep on her shoulder, with the green kerchief still in his mouth.

The moon was partially masked by heavy clouds, sending spiky fingers into the dark trees.

'It's a helluva way,' moaned Jake-Wayne. 'This is a god-awful state.'

'You watch your mouth, boy,' said Ma.

Jake-Wayne put his chin on his chest and sulked.

'Look,' she hissed, pointing her bony finger ahead. '*The oaks*. I remember the avenue of oaks.' The tall trees were guarding the old house, sheltering it from prying eyes, but Cody drove past them with little reverence to their significance. 'It's a long avenue, I was here as a young lady,' quipped Ma.

'You were never young,' said Jake-Wayne. 'Young people know how to have fun.'

'I've had fun,' said Ma.

The car lights flickered as they picked up scurrying beetles in the dust, which had begun swirling in front of them. The fallen leaves from the oaks whirled like they were being sucked down a plughole. Branches swayed as the wind whipped, tossing more leaves into the wash.

'Where'd that weather come from all of a sudden?' asked Cody.

'Hey, I don't like this,' screamed Jake-Wayne as the car began to rattle.

What seemed like a bullet hit the windscreen, followed by another and another. One made a dent in the driver's door.

'Help, I don't want to die,' the boy shouted.

The baby woke, his lungs pumping out his need for food.

The right-side passenger door flew open almost sucking Jake-Wayne right out, but he managed to grab on to Ma. He looked into her beady eyes – pleading. It was then he began to slide sideways from his seat. His fingernails dug into Ma's thin arm through her cotton dress. Little drops of red showed through the white – but in a swoosh Jake-Wayne had gone. The car door slammed shut with a clunk. The wind died.

Inside the still car there was stunned silence.

Ma broke the hush. 'Jake-Wayne's okay, he'll be back when he's better.' She looked directly into Lily-May's saucer-eyes.

Louanna gaped over her shoulder at Ma who now stared at the back of Cody's bald head.

'Right, Cody,' whispered the old woman, 'time to see what's in the big house… drive on.'

# The Tree Museum

'Grandma, do you think God is in nature?'

'I'm not answering that on the grounds it might incriminate me.'

'I do.'

'Be careful, Toni, walls have ears you know. Even glass ones like this.'

'But, Grandma, this must be born of God. What's its name?'

'Iridaceous family.'

'We're not allowed to study Latin anymore.'

'It's a crocus.'

'Crocus… it's lovely.'

'We had a lot of crocuses back then.'

'Do you miss it, Grandma?'

'Miss what? My youth?'

'No, the crocuses in, what was it called? A…'

'Garden.'

'Yes, the crocuses and the garden.'

'I do, Toni. I miss the honeyed smell of the roses. But the summer of 2142 was the beginning of the end. The roses were the first to go.'

'Do they have roses here?'

'No. Someone managed to save roses in The Devon Quarter, I think.'

'When *they* came?'

'Yes, keep your voice down, Toni! I would like to get home tonight.'

'It's all right, Grandma, the rays can't get through the glass.'

'Don't you believe it! They cauterised Jacob Bell's tongue in the bread queue.'

'Oh! That made me shiver, like someone just walked on my grave.'

'Toni, *they* will if you're not more careful. Look, here's the arboretum.'

'Grandma, this is lovely. It feels so cool. So... do you believe in God?'

'Toni, please don't.'

'But look at this magnificent tree with its feathered leaves and its gnarled bark and tell me God isn't here.'

'Look outside. How could your God do that?'

'But he kept these specimens for us to look at.'

'No, He didn't, Toni, we Alphas did.'

'Grandma?'

'There, now I've said too much. It's getting dark, let's go. Don't forget your helmet, and telepath your mother that we are coming home.'

'I just did. Grandma, I'll pray to God again tonight to help us all.'

'Does He ever answer you?'

'Not yet, but He will one day.'

'I hope so, Toni.'

'He will, Grandma, He will.'

# One Hour

'One hour,' they said. I'm not even sure what one hour is any more.

'Look at the little hand on the clock, when it moves to the next number you have to come back,' they said.

I agreed but with some trepidation. This was my first time. My journey was quick, so that was good.

The door was open. A gentle breeze rustled the orange, silk petals of the ornamental flowers arranged on the hall table. I smiled. They'd been there the last time I was here. I went in. Looking around, nothing much had changed. Two coats hung on the rack: one green and one blue. Both smelled of Polo Mints.

Off the long, grey, carpeted hallway were four doors. I thought I would find them behind the last door. The one that was ajar. I peeped in. Fast asleep but on her own. I hoped not to wake her and just watched.

She looked so small, alone in that huge brown chair. I wanted to take her in my arms and squeeze her like I used to do. She looked too frail to squeeze now, as if she might break. Her skin was thin, almost translucent.

I watched the veins pulsing in her sallow arms. Arms that used to hold me close when I'd fallen off my bike as a kid. Her tiny hands were all gnarled and wizened. They couldn't stroke my cheeks and brush the tears away now, but how I wished they could. She stirred, so I moved back.

Settling again, she instinctively rubbed her arms, as if she were cold, then moved her silver-flecked candy-floss head to the left. Her rhythmical breathing returned. I wondered if she'd been dreaming.

The clock. I'd forgotten it. I frantically searched. Where was the clock? My hunt took me to the sideboard. Do people still call them sideboards? I'm not sure, but it's what they called it. The top was still full of photographs.

Snapshots of memories. I was six, in a sticky out yellow frock. White ankle socks and a ribbon in my bobbed, brown hair. Big smile. Happy. Thoughts of Whit Sunday parades came flooding back. I was a Guide at twelve. A black and white picture showed me holding the flag at the front of a procession. Reverend Wyatt took that one. He was a good man. Talked a lot of sense – thankfully. Helped me believe.

But no clock. A wave of panic began to ripple through me.

It must be on the wall. I scanned. And caught sight of a large portrait I'd never seen before. A young woman with bright blue eyes and long brunette hair. A pointed-up nose and rose lipped smile. They must have had that done after I'd left. Perhaps someone painted it from a photo? They'd done it well. Made me look quite human. My skin never looked that good. Nice glow. It must have been taken before I was twenty-seven. Surprisingly, I was on my motorbike.

A chime. It came from the hall. I rushed to look. A draught closed the door. I fixed it with a stare. There was no sound from inside the room. Why did I do that? I'll have to let her sleep now.

The big finger was on the six and the little finger just past the two. Did that mean I had to go when it reached three? It didn't seem long enough.

I looked out of the hallway window. A figure was hunched over a garden border. He was still. I felt myself tense, anxious. Then, he jerked, and up came a dandelion, root, and all, flying through the air. He was waving his trowel and shouting at the invading flower. It fell on the long, straggly, grass.

*You're next*, I thought. *He will be giving you a 'haircut' soon.*

He levered himself gingerly off the ground and sure enough walked towards the shed, where he used to keep the lawnmower.

I ventured up the stairs. Thirteen of them. We used to count them when I was little. They'd pull me up the stairs singing, *Yo, Heave Ho!* It was some kind of Russian military song, I think. I loved it.

I loved bedtime, because once I'd snuggled down under my candy-striped flannel sheets and pink, candlewick bedspread, he would tell me stories. His brown eyes smiled, and the stories poured out. His voice was like drinking hot chocolate. Jason, who searched for the Golden Fleece and Icarus who flew too close to the sun so that his wings melted.

'Always do things with caution,' he said, waggling his finger at me.

I should have listened.

My bedroom door was shut. I didn't go in.

'Phyl! Are you there, love?'

That shout made me jump.

His voice at the bottom of the stairs. He was in his gardening clogs. White slip-ons with holes in and, of course, socks. Black socks. His trousers were rolled up to his bony knees, revealing pads to stop them from hurting, as he

51

tended to his borders and his roses. He loved his roses. Digging and potashing and greenflying. We used to do them together sometimes. He taught me how to use secateurs. She always used to put her hands over her eyes when she saw me doing it.

'Always cut downwards,' he'd say. 'And only a quarter of an inch from the bud.'

I had no idea what a quarter of an inch was but revelled in that smile he gave me when I'd finished and looked to him for approval. I'm glad he still looks after his roses.

He didn't look upstairs. 'Brr... it's cold in here,' he said blowing on his hands. 'Phyl, are you awake?' He hobbled into the living room and I followed.

Mum was rubbing her eyes.

'I had a lovely dream about Becky. I dreamt she came to visit.'

'I've cut her a rose from the remembrance bush,' said Dad. 'It smells just like she used to do.' He held it out for Mum.

'Gorgeous,' she said. She lifted the delicate white rose up to her nose and drank in the scent. There was a moment of silence, then, 'We'll put it on the mantle under her picture.' Mum kissed the rose and placed it in a little glass vase.

Dad's arms enveloped her, and he laid his head on her back.

'She would have been thirty-seven today.' He sighed.

The clock in the hallway pinged.

*No! It's too soon.* I wanted to join in the hug and tell them I'm okay. But my time was up. I looked around the room for one last time, blew them a kiss and whispered, '*I love you.*'

The petals on the rose in the little glass vase quivered.

When I got back, Saint Christopher had his hands on his hips and that look on his face.

Francis smiled. 'Just made it,' he said, and I smiled back.

'It was special. Thank you for letting me go.'

Saint Peter locked the gates and placed his arm around my slumped shoulders. 'Don't be sad, Becky. It won't be too long. You'll all be together again soon.'

# When Spring Is Lost

And when we met it was the buds of spring
that began unfurling then, tight folds now
loosened their hold and birds began to sing
a song of joy, upon a blossomed bough.

A skip, lamb-like, followed my lover's kiss,
Whilst the grass grew green and lush, ripe for love
we found ourselves, and bloomed in sultry bliss,
Sweet was the cherry that dropped from above.

But can a love sustain when brown leaves fall
and the thatch turns hoary with silver frost,
Will the honey taste bitter with the call
of winter, that waits when the spring is lost?

The tree holds its bent hand out to show how,
A love can be young, though we're older now.

# Pelvic Thrusts at the U3A

I've been looking forward to this all day. *Pelvic Thrust Work Out,* the advert at the gym said. I haven't had a pelvic thrust work out since I ditched *Prostate Derek.*

'Cruel,' Mother said.

Mind you, I hear he's now courting Mandy Kinsey. Maybe she's not too worried about pelvic thrusts. A good dinner companion and someone to go down *The Legion* with are all some over-seventies want. Me, I can't wait to watch Melvin teaching us U3A members how to thrust. He's got a look of a middle-aged Usain Bolt. I'm wearing Lycra. Hope he does.

Mother couldn't come. 'I've got a touch of Sisyphus,' she said. I had visions of boulders up hills and Greek togas but told her that cranberry juice always works for me and I'll fetch her some after the class.

This gymnasium smells like a cross between a three-week-old, unwashed jockstrap and the cheese stall at Borough Market. A positively hybrid Jockfort. I open the windows to much moaning from Carrie Wimpole.

'It's freezing in here,' she whines, clearly oblivious to the pong of the bastard child of a surgical support and a French cheese.

I mutter under my breath, 'Wear a vest then.' And begin to limber up. This consists of me sitting on a work bench. Putting my trainers on. Getting my upper torso over the jelly that is now my belly requires some doing, and I consider that to be 'stretches'. It hurts enough, so that'll do for me.

I see Vincent Coombes has turned up. All black crackling tracksuit and white pumps. The static coming off him as he walks makes him look like a Van Der Graaff generator. I mustn't stand next to him when he takes his jacket off – might blow my pacemaker.

That's interesting; Malcolm Jenks has pitched up too. It's not very often we see him nowadays. He's been keeping himself to himself. Well, the rumour from Mother is… that he's been seen out with another woman.

'It's hardly five months since Mary passed and he's already on the tiles, like a dirty dog on heat,' Mother said.

I smile *hello* to Kulwinder. She's got a large plastic box under her arm. My mouth salivates at the thought of her minced samosas. She often brings a little something she is trying out to classes. At the last *Sumo Wrestling for Beginners* class, it was Saag Gosht with a twist. Ratufa Indica, Google said. Giant squirrel. It would have been better had she brought some spoons.

Malcolm sidles up between us and gives Kulwinder a wink. He bends down, showing off, trying to touch his toes. There's a rasp and I think he's torn his leggings, but the puff of air from his derriere carries Keema Naan and Lamb Rogan Josh on it, confirmation that it's Kulwinder he's been 'Kama-Sutra-ing'. Wait till I tell Mother.

Melvin enters the room with a flourish. My fantasies are fulfilled – he's wearing tight Lycra, and I can see he's brought his lunch box too. The purple sweat socks and matching headband are good. Rhianna's *Rude Boy* begins to play; I push to the front of the hall and Melvin thrusts.

I feel light-headed. He walks round the room encouragingly, moving people's hips back and forth. In anticipation of my turn, I work up quite a sweat. Thank God for *Tena Pants*. He stops behind Vincent. There's a definite spark from his trackie bottoms to Melvin's silky, stretched, purple thighs.

'Come on, rude boy, can you get it up?' Melvin sings along with Rhianna, as he manipulates *static boy's* hips in sync with his own.

I am sooo disappointed. Another one to tell Mother about.

I think I'll swerve this class next week – I might try mixed touch rugby instead.

# Catastrophe in Chipping Clayton

Sister Francis Copolla of the Order of Saint Gordon and the Holy Martyrs was arrested yesterday and charged with the abduction of several cats. The cats, all ginger toms, belonged to the local vicars of the Parish of Lower Clayton.

The felines all went missing on Friday nights. Something that Inspector Dick Husband of Dullchester Police found intriguing. 'I knew this was a serial abductor, after the third cat in a row went missing on a Friday night,' he said to the press gathered outside Bodge Street police station.

Sister Francis is a well-known figure in the area. Riding her bike around the parish, she could often be seen with her robes tucked into her undergarments, presumably to stop them getting caught in her bicycle chain.

Local publican Harry Chambers remembers seeing her on one particular Friday night and he became suspicious. 'I was just slopping out the drip trays into the roses, when I heard a repeated creak, that sounded like an un-oiled bicycle wheel. And when I looked up there was Sister Francis with something up her habit – well, it was either that or she'd eaten too many pies. I shouted hello but she ignored me and rode off towards the abbey,' he said.

Fortunately, the cats have since been returned to their owners and all are in good health. However, the three local vicars affected by this catnapping episode are reportedly seeking damages from Sister Francis, as all three toms were returned minus certain body parts – namely their testicles.

'I am devastated,' said Father Gerry O'Gorman, when asked how he felt about the operations the nun had allegedly performed. 'She has robbed me of my right to choose.'

Father Patrick Callaghan was in tears. 'I hope my tom had anaesthetic,' he wailed.

Sister Francis was held at an undisclosed location overnight to protect her from the frenzy of male protesters rallying on the station steps. She'll appear in court on Friday.

*Reported by Charlene Sniffer for the Chipping Clayton Chronicle.*

# Are They Your Red Shoes?

Are they your red shoes that you wore that day, when they took you away
    from all you knew?

promise of life in the east, when your mother gave them her keys, and lifted
    you onto that train,

a journey to death, did you hold your breath against the vile smells, which
    came from men,

your little case packed with knick-knacks, and ribbons and toys that you
    would never hold again,

the window slats shut in that hut, on the line that took you to your final
    destination, at that station,

blinking in the sunlight, with your curls held tight by a bow that matched
    your hopeful red shoes,

your bag held close to your chest, but then you had to leave it like the rest,
    on that crowded platform,

told to march on with your mum, and the others, to leave your brothers and
    turn left not right,

and into the night, with no stars in the sky and no passers-by to see what
    was happening there,

did they take your shoes then, when you waited for showers in those dark
    hours with no light?

*Why...*

all men and women need to open their eyes, and cry, that this was allowed
     by looking away,
your red shoes are there, to bear witness so, we all know, that what
     happened to you was true.

# Marie

'Now stay down, you mare,' snarled Mam, as Marie fell to the floor clutching her already swelling face.

There was a snigger from the other room. Jed was pleased. That was just where he liked his daughter – on the floor.

'You all right, mam?' he shouted from the fat-stinking kitchen of the two-up two-down, scruffy terraced house in Manchester.

'Yeah, I am now!' she crowed.

Marie knew it was for the best that she stayed down.

'I'm sick of you, Marie, you ruin my life,' slurred Mam, from where she had collapsed on the brown velour sofa.

Marie knew this; she was told often enough.

Yesterday, Marie had understood what she must do with her secret.

She curled up into a foetal ball. She could taste her own fear.

Mam flicked her cigarette ash onto her stepdaughter's head. The TV's noise continued but all Marie could hear was the clock ticking.

Six more hours – then she would be released.

The pans crashed in the sink and Marie jumped. Not a good sound but she stayed down. She pulled her knees closer to her chin. Jed's boot caught her on the side of her stomach. She instinctively cradled it.

They chinked their glasses. 'Cheers.'

Marie could smell the fetid whisky. Eventually, a glass slipped to the floor. The endgame was near.

The clock ticked and ticked and ticked.

As if it didn't dare to look, a chink of light peeped through the tatty grey curtains.

From her pocket, Marie pulled out a black and white scan picture. She kissed it and slipped it into her school shirt, next to her heart.

Outside the dawn air was clean. A robin with a worm in its mouth, perched on a fence post, head cocked, watching Marie. She clasped her suitcase to her chest, breathed deeply and stepped through the gate.

Satisfied, the robin flew away.

# Under the Stairs

Petey snuggled up next to Mae's skirt. She stroked his soft brown hair.

'Thanks for coming,' she said.

The shouting continued outside, and Mae heard a crash.

'So, how's your day been?' she asked.

Petey was quiet. They sat in silence for a while.

'I've had another crap day,' Mae eventually said.

Petey sat back and looked at her.

'Yeah, late again and a detention for not having the right coloured shoes on. They're all full of bull at that school. What do they know about shoes? My black shoes pinch my toes, and my trainers are the only other ones I've got.'

Petey looked at his own un-shod feet.

A bottle hit a wall and it sounded like a thousand pieces fell on the tiled floor.

Petey sniffed.

Mae could smell the gin.

'Not nice is it? I tasted it once. It's rank. Gave me a headache in the morning but I slept well. Missed school that morning too.' She laughed. 'I'll stick to the cider I think.'

Mae was cold, so she pulled the blanket over her arms. She was glad she'd remembered to bring it this time. She tucked the threadbare cover around Petey. He looked up at her with shiny eyes.

'Okay?' she asked.

Mae opened her book and adjusted the torch so that the words were illuminated. She read Petey a chapter from *The Amber Spy Glass* by Philip Pullman.

It was about 10 o'clock by the time the noise subsided. She had learnt to judge the time by the silence. They'd be asleep. Mae would be sure to creep up to her room, avoiding the creaky stair.

Petey had long gone. He'd taken the cheese and gone back through the hole to feed his family.

Mae stretched herself through the open door and stood up. She winced, and twisted her back, left, and right. Picking up the blanket, she quietly closed the cupboard door and headed up to her room. Remembering to step over the *tell-tale* stair.

# Jacko's Story

The pot hit the wall and the force loosened its lid. Red paint sploshed over nearby windows and pieces of fruit laid out on a plate. Jacko watched the faces of the adults as they turned towards him. They looked black. He wasn't sure what they were going to do so he just stood and watched.

The next thing he remembered was his mother sitting behind the glass of the fat woman's room. He wasn't sure how she'd got in there and his tummy hurt thinking that she wouldn't get out. He'd tried the handle before, and it didn't open the door. He sat on the chair where he was told to sit, which was okay because it was blue.

He watched his mother's mouth open and close and the fat woman's eyebrows move up and down. His mother stood up quickly and opened the door. Jacko thought she was very clever to know how to do that, when the handle didn't work.

In the car on the way home the only sound he could hear was crying.

When he got to the house, Jacko went to his desk and took his magnifying glass into the garden. He lay on his front in the long grass of the wildflower patch that his mother had helped him sow and looked for arachnids. He wanted to test his theory that he could find three different types of arachnids by the time his mother called him in for food.

He was still searching when a very tall man wearing glasses, with a bushy beard and hair sticking out of his ears, came into the garden. The man sat down at the wrought iron table, where Jacko liked to read his guides to spiders, insects, or butterflies. He studied the dark suit and tie carefully. The man might be okay – the clothes were grey.

His mother brought out cups and a pot on a tray and put it on the table. She spoke to the man who nodded his head. His mother poured something in the cups. The man took a pad from his black leather bag, and a pen from a green case that he had put on the table.

Jacko felt calm so he carried on investigating arachnids.

'So, Mrs Birch, how long has Jacko been at nursery school?' asked the man.

'Since the day after his third birthday,' she replied. 'Four weeks.'

'And they've excluded him already?' he said.

'Yes, the Headmistress said the paint incident was the last straw.'

'Can you fill me in on what occurred before the incident with the paint pot?' the man asked, raising his cup to his lips.

From the safety of the long grass, Jacko spied him blowing into the cup. Jacko wondered why a candle would be in the man's cup.

'Well, the first thing was the refusal to sit on his allocated chair. They tried to insist he did, and he threw it. It didn't hit anyone, but he was beside himself when I got there. I couldn't console him.'

'When was this, Mrs Birch?' he asked.

'Day one,' she said.

Jacko thought about the day of the flying chair. He'd had to get it away from himself as fast as he could, and he knew throwing was a good way of moving something quickly. He'd been to the park with his father and they had thrown a ball. His father called him *dead-eyed Jacko,* which he said meant he was good at throwing, not that he had a dead eye.

He had been at the park a long time with his father and it had given him a nice feeling in his tummy. The people at nursery didn't give him that nice feeling. Not that day. They were noisy, so Jacko put his fingers in his ears and screamed to shut their noise out.

The tall man with the bushy beard and hairs in his ears talked to Jacko's mother. Jacko looked at him through his magnifying glass. The man's face changed shape and Jacko was frightened, so he threw the glass at him.

'Jacko, no!' shouted his mother.

'It's all right,' said the man. 'No harm done.'

Jacko sat on the edge of the garden decking and he heard her tell him about the time he refused to hold a girl's hand in the playground. She had those things on her hands that were the colour of the gooey stuff that came out of his nose, so he wouldn't touch them.

His mother told the man about the beans and tomato sauce on his plate at lunchtime, and how he had tipped them onto the floor. But he'd wanted to eat his fish cake and he couldn't with that scary mess on the plate. The adults had funny faces and the fat woman shouted at him that day.

His father came out of the house. Jacko thought it must be 5.55 as that was the time his father came home from work. His father shook hands with the tall man in the dark suit. Jacko sat back on his heels; his brain was fuzzy.

He hadn't had his food yet and his father was home. His tummy rumbled. He started to get hot, so he took off his T-shirt.

'So, when did you begin to notice the change in Jacko's behaviour?' the man asked Jacko's father.

'Well, I would say not long after he was two,' Jacko's father said. He turned to smile at Jacko.

Jacko was now back in the long grass, lying on his back, holding a struggling spider up to the light to count its legs.

'That's right,' said his mother. 'It was after he came out of hospital. He'd had a ridiculous temperature and a febrile convulsion, I think they call it, so he was admitted to hospital. He had terrible nose bleeds. He was in for about five days and after he came out, we noticed these little things.'

Jacko could hear everything that was said. He shivered, remembering his time in hospital. In his head he saw strips of lights that flickered on and off and green curtains that closed around his bed, making him think he was a caterpillar in a cocoon. His mother sat next to his bed and she looked white. His sheets were white, except when they went red. Jacko shivered again.

'Yes,' said Jacko's father. 'Like refusing to wear his *Fireman Sam* pyjamas and screaming at the sight of his engines. He wouldn't look at the *Name the Colour* book we bought him, and once he threw it at Diane's head.'

'He has no friends,' said his mother. 'The nursery says he laughs when children fall over. They don't want to play with him. It's as if he doesn't know how to make friends.'

Jacko saw his mother take a piece of paper out of her pocket and put it to her eyes. His father went to her and put his arm on her shoulder and his mother wiped her eyes on his father's shirt.

'He plays with his cousin, Caleb,' said his father.

'No, Jacko plays at him,' said Jacko's mother. 'He flies his aeroplanes at him, and drives his trains at him, he doesn't play *with* him.'

'Do they talk to each other?' the man said.

Jacko's mother said, 'No.'

Jacko knew about his cousin, Caleb — because his mother took him to visit Caleb's house. Jacko knew Caleb lived at 94 Brighton Crescent. The house had a green door, yellow curtains at the windows, and a carpet that he could drop his cars on with no crash. Jacko liked it there. A woman called Aunty Julie lived there with Caleb. The house was quiet. There wasn't any music banging. Sometimes Aunty Julie made him cakes and let him lick the spoon. Caleb licked the spoon too. Once Aunty Julie gave Jacko a book about ants. He put it under his pillow on his bed.

Jacko sat up and studied the man with the beard. His eyes were shiny behind his glasses as he stared at his mother and father. His face was still. Jacko figured he must be sad. What they were saying made the man sad.

Jacko knew the word sad from his short time at nursery. He was told he had made Molly Jones sad when he wouldn't hold her hand in the playground game. She wouldn't take her hand-things off and that made Jacko's tummy ache. Jacko began to rock. He rocked so that his tummy would feel better.

His mother spoke again. 'Unfortunately, once he got hold of a pair of scissors from the kitchen table. He was waving them around and I told him *not to be silly*, so he marched out into the garden and he cut all the heads off the poppies in the flower patch. I said he had to pick them up, but he went into a complete meltdown. He was screaming and running around the garden. I couldn't control him. My neighbour, Mrs Derby, popped her head over the fence and asked me what on earth was going on.'

Jacko looked up from his hand where a spider was making its way from his thumb across the palm, while he was listening to the conversation. The man would have to spend a long time telling his mother what was happening on the earth. He liked transport and could name lots of things that were going on the earth, like buses and trains and cars and taxis and cranes and…

Jacko's father came up to him, bent down and asked how he was feeling.

Jacko knew he was feeling hot.

'What are you doing, buddy?' his father said.

Jacko looked over his shoulder. He thought his father must have changed the dog's name to Buddy. He remembered it used to be called Chas. Chas wasn't there.

*He must be in the kitchen,* thought Jacko, and wandered into the house to find him, leaving his father open-mouthed.

The dog was in the kitchen eating from his bowl. He gave Jacko a warm feeling in his tummy, especially when he put his head on Jacko's legs and rubbed himself there. Once Jacko was lying on the kitchen floor because it was cool on his back, and the dog came over and licked his face. It felt wet and warm. Jacko had looked at the dog and his tongue had fallen out of his mouth. A pain had shot through Jacko's tummy and he'd closed his eyes. The dog stroked Jacko's face with his head.

Inside his brain, Jacko had talked to himself. *Pink is okay, pink is okay,* he'd repeated. When he'd felt calm, he opened his eyes and the dog was still there looking at him, with his pink tongue sticking out. The dog waited for a long time until Jacko stroked his head. The pain in his tummy went away and the warm feeling came.

Jacko sat and watched the dog eat his dinner and his tummy rumbled again. He knew his mother often got his own food out of the fridge, but he couldn't reach the door handle. She had moved the biscuits from the drawers, where he used to help himself, into a high cupboard, after the time he had eaten two packets of biscuits. She had a black face and shouted at him for giving the dog some. Jacko didn't understand why, as they had a picture of a dog on the packet. He reached into the dog's bowl and grabbed a handful of meat. The dog didn't even move, so Jacko knew it was okay.

After he'd had his dinner, Jacko came back into the garden. He was naked. He felt burning hot, so he'd taken off his shorts and pants to cool himself down. His mother shouted at him to put his clothes on this instant, but he didn't know where this instant was, so he stayed still and waited until she told him.

The tall man with the glasses, stood up.

'Okay, Mr and Mrs Birch, I will see Jacko at the assessment clinic on Thursday 4th November at 1 o'clock. There will be a letter in the post. I am sure we will be able to help him… and you. One last question if I may – what was the cause of Jacko's febrile convulsion – did the hospital say?'

'Yes, they said it was probably caused by his vaccinations the day before,' said Jacko's father.

'Ah, I see,' said the man.

Jacko was glad that the tall man could see, it meant his glasses worked right.

# Special Knight

He always came in the night when he could. I snuggled down under my cherry pink and yellow patchwork bedspread, pretending to be asleep. The door would creak… that's when I couldn't contain myself.

My eyes flew open and out of my mouth came, 'Another story pleeeeease.' (Dad was a sucker for soft soap). Inevitably there would be 'just one more,' and I had him to myself.

Dad was away a lot during my childhood, so times spent with him were special. The Gulf War and the Bosnian War interrupted my formative years. Mum was often left with just me and my brother for company. She did her best to hold down a full-time job and bring us up 'proper', as she used to say, but there wasn't much time or energy for reading stories. And when Dad was home, she had her hands full. She worked extra hard to make him happier.

My dad loved myths and legends from the Egyptians. He used to tell me about Amun Ra, King of the Gods, and Osiris, who was chopped into pieces by his brother, and how Cleopatra had killed herself with an asp. Dad held the books open but didn't turn many pages, yet the stories poured out. His voice was like melted chocolate. My heart felt full. His eyes twinkled in the dim night light, and it was then he smiled most.

'Special nights,' I said at his funeral. 'Precious times.'

My brother nodded in his front row pew. Mum just bowed her head and shakily held on to her son's hand. My brother read a poem that Dad had taught him about a knight in search of Eldorado.

The gallant knight rode long and hard in his quest but couldn't find what he was looking for. The poem then tells of a shadow falling over his heart as he realised Eldorado was unobtainable.

It was then that we all wept.

# I Was You Once

Hey, up there, can you hear me, or do your ears need aids?
Can you see me from your high horse, or are you blind as well?
Can you smell me from that distance? Perhaps, I've not had a wash in weeks,
Step lightly there and you won't touch me – then I won't even exist.
I was you once, so I get it
but now there's only me -
and my blanket
and my box
and my dog
and my tin,
please put some money in
it says, on the label that I wrote.
I can write, I went to school,
I can read, I use the library -
especially in the winter,
I was good at maths, at fifteen or so
I passed all my exams,
there was a path laid out -
but I zigged instead of zagged.
At home I learnt to hide -
a head above the parapet,

gets hit,
so, I stayed away, and my mother couldn't find me.
I ran so I could be
and breathe
and live and be free -
but only at night,
with my blanket, that keeps me warm
and my box, that shelters
and my dog, who loves unconditionally
and my tin – that confirms me.
I was you once, so I get it
but just this time…
Can you listen, now?
Can you look me in the eye?
Can you close your nose to the smell that galls?
Can you step towards me – this time?
Then maybe I'll remember
That – I do exist.
I was you once.

# Sherrington Woods

The thing I most liked about Sherrington Woods was the colour in the fading sun of late autumn. Copper and dun were woven together to lay a patterned carpet along our path.

The early mornings, when Jack had waved his spiky fingers, crisping the edges of each rustic leaf. Where white webs that were woven overnight wrapped themselves round our faces, sticky and clinging and complex. It makes me shiver now.

But it was the surprise of the hoary headed mushrooms, unexpectedly emerging through the earth in the damp shade of the leaden oak, which reminds me of you. And what was.

'Hello, Jessy, how are you?' A voice interrupts my thoughts.

'I'm good, David,' I reply.

'I'm loving your painting, Jessy. It's really taking shape now.'

'Yes,' I say.

David means well, but he doesn't understand. No one will ever understand.

'Do you have all the colours that you need?' he asks.

'Sure,' I give.

*Red is red is red, I think – except when it's scarlet.*

I need David to leave me alone now. He usually does, wafting off to go and help some other deserving soul. I must get this bit right. His eyes dart around the room. He does this all the time. Today there are only four of us, so he shouldn't be so uptight. Lauren is sick. And that's the truth. Unfortunately, that means he'll have more time for me.

Yellow and red makes orange, like fire. The story of our relationship really. You mellow yellow and me blood red. Then you turned grey. Fungus-like. Sucking the colour out of me.

I bought a cherry red hair dye, just like in that photo you secreted in your bedside drawer. The one with the scarlet lipstick kiss on it.

But you didn't like it.

'It's not you,' you said.

*It's not her,* you meant. So, I went back to black and made vermillion lines on my arms instead.

'Does the pallet knife help with the texture, Jessy?' David again from across the room.

'Yes, thank you.'

The broad blade spreads the thick claret colour across the sienna, just like it did that day. Oozing and mingling and pooling on the orange and brown rusty splashed carpet.

I can see David approaching from the corner of my eye and I know what he's going to say.

'Oh, you've spoiled your painting, Jessy.'

Just as I'd anticipated, so I lift the knife.
He hits the red button, and they come for me.
I'll start the painting again, next time I'm allowed out.
Sherrington Woods was so lovely.

# Look at the Stars

The lyrics from the *Coldplay* song seeped through the damp night.

Cory smirked. It seemed appropriate that song had been selected on the pub jukebox. He could hear it in his garden because the pub's French doors were wedged open. He blew cigarette smoke into the night sky. It formed a grey swirl against the black. Cory flicked the end of the cigarette into a bush and turned his jacket collar up to protect his neck, then rubbed his chilled hands together.

*Someone will shut the doors soon; it will be closing time. Then there will be no more music. The lights will go out and this little idyll I've found for Molly and me will be completely dark.* This time Cory's smirk became a silent laugh.

He'd moved Molly here from inner city Manchester. Dirty, grimy, far too busy, people-nosying Manchester, he thought – but Molly was reluctant to give it up.

'No, I'll miss my mam,' she argued when he first asked her to come. She'd already had the trauma of losing her dad, Ron, the year before, in an unfortunate car accident.

'Faulty brakes,' the inquest had said.

Cory shook his head.

It was only six months after Cory had begged Molly to move to the country with him that Molly's mother Jacqueline had died of food poisoning. Cory shuddered at the pain and sickness that he and Molly endured too. A take-away curry had been blamed. But they were younger than Jacqueline and survived. He wrapped his arms around his body, just like he had done to Molly that day, promising he would protect her from the rest of the world. He'd carried her over the threshold of their country idyll two months later.

And life was idyllic. He worked in his study, building websites for people with more money than sense, and Molly would bring him coffee and hunks of home-made bread, warm from the oven.

Cory licked his lips, and his breath froze in the night air. He shivered. He could hear the last of the pub's regulars starting their cars. Drinking and driving. Common in the countryside. Cory tutted. The sound seemed magnified and he startled himself. He looked around in the dark, but no one was there.

He lit another cigarette and looked at the pub lights, willing them to go out, so that he could have pitch-black. He liked it, along with the peace and quiet, and only him and Molly in her apron.

Molly didn't. 'Bored,' she'd said. 'Miss the action,' she'd said. So, she got herself a part-time job as a barmaid.

'I love it,' she told him after the first night, when Cory had sat waiting.

It wasn't long till she was having a drink after work with the other bar staff, and still Cory sat and waited, listening to the music die down and for the key in the latch. He was there with the milk on the hob ready to pour on the cocoa, but one day the milk had boiled dry and the pan burnt.

He had gone to the car park. The pub lights were out but the moonlit silhouettes didn't lie.

Cory had bided his time. Planned things properly like he'd done with Ron and Jacqueline. Another drunk driver and a tricky bend in a country road. He knew Molly had gone to the funeral.

'Well, he was a regular,' she'd said.

Cory told her she needed a holiday when he'd found her crying the next day.

'New Zealand, I've booked it. Six months,' Cory had said. He'd smiled at her showing his teeth. The suitcases were at the front door.

The last pub light flicked off. Cory looked into the black. The stars seemed to become more lucent.

He looked down at Molly lying on the cold damp earth.

'Are you looking at the stars, Molly?' he asked his dead wife. He began to softly hum the *Coldplay* tune and he picked up the spade.

# The Window

Staring out of the window, I see tears streaming down the reflection. It can't be me; I know how to hide my pain. One drop crawls towards another and they clasp at each other, forming a rivulet. It pools and then falls off the edge of the sill.

The storm is as fierce as forecasted, and yet it has such a pretty name – Fleur. She's certainly battered her own namesake. Some early spring daffodils are bowing their heads away from the wind like shy maids, as if they have something to hide.

The tall, bearded trees are shaking with anger and the logs in the woodpile are sodden. They should have had a better shelter. The axe is off its stand and has been thrown to the floor, it will need sharpening now. Grey fists have formed in the sky. It looks as if they are trying to out-fight each other. A fork of light splits them, and just for a moment they halt their battle, and then resume their sparring to thunderous applause.

I pull my cardigan tighter round my chest. My sticky fingers touch the back of my neck. I think someone has just walked over my grave and I know why.

Moving away from the window I look at the boxes. I hadn't kept to the rules very well. There are too many memories poking up over the rims. They're probably too heavy to lift, but I haven't got the energy to do it again.

The letters are on the mantelpiece, the one for my daughter Caroline on top, the other one hidden behind it. They can have that, it will be useful. I don't need to read it again.

The car will be here soon. Even in this storm I'm sure they'll hurry. I take up my position by the window to watch them arrive. The rain is almost horizontal now and has sheared one of the heads off the daffodils. Storm Fleur's pent-up anger seems vengeful.

A pair of big yellow eyes head up the driveway. They don't screech to a halt like they do in the movies and there is no flashing blue light. I feel slightly disappointed. Two men in long raincoats step out of the car and try to shield themselves from the storm, but Fleur is taking no prisoners today.

My hands have dried now, making my fingers feel crusty, so I rub them together, and tiny claret-coloured flakes flutter to the carpet. I slip the latch, let them in, and stare at their sopping wet shoes. They look at my red feet.

'He's in there,' I say.

They tread on my gooey and now rust coloured Axminster with their wet shoes. Observing the packing boxes, one of them retches into his handkerchief.

'Not many men carry a handkerchief nowadays,' I say.

They look at me open-mouthed.

'What happened here, love?' one asks.

'Read the letter,' I reply.

# The Guest House

There was that fluttering again. She wasn't sure if it was in the room, or her heart beating in her ears. She looked up to the loft space in the attic, not that she could see much, now the power had failed. Where was the proprietor with the promised candles? The only light was from her mobile phone.

This was just typical of the day she'd had. She'd given a crap presentation to the brewery company, the hotel she thought she had booked had no record of her reservation, and now here she was in this ramshackle bed and breakfast in the middle of nowhere – with a power failure. She thought about checking her phone to make sure it wasn't Friday the 13th.

There were footsteps on the stairs. Great. Mr Brown the owner must have found the candles. The footsteps stopped… but no knock at the door? She heard a latch being drawn back and almost a whoosh as something dropped, but it didn't hit the floor.

She felt almost blinded by the darkness. There weren't even any streetlights to help. Her breathing became rapid and she struggled to control it. She decided to phone Darren and tell him what had happened and where she was, hearing a human voice would help.

Beep, beep… beep… was the only sound she heard – her mobile had run out of battery.

*Oh no, please no.*

She moved away from the window. The dark was now all consuming and she was disorientated. Hitting her leg against a chair, she cursed her luck again. She knew she shouldn't have used the phone as a satnav. If she had chosen differently, she wouldn't have found this god-awful place and the phone battery wouldn't be flat.

The fluttering was there again, this time directly above her. She realised she must be under the loft hatch.

*Maybe a pigeon has got in there and can't escape?*

Beads of sweat formed on her top lip. The fluttering she thought was in her ears was now a pounding. She tried to find the door. Feeling for the chair – she knew the bed would be next – her fingers touched the duvet.

*Okay,* she thought, *the door is opposite the bed.*

With arms reaching out, she slid one foot in front of the other, in the direction of the door. It seemed like an age before she found it. Exhaling, she quickly turned the brass handle one way, then the other. She rattled the door, pushing and pulling it at the same time. It was locked.

Behind her she heard the loft hatch being slowly slid back, and that familiar whoosh from the hole in the ceiling.

Banging on the door, she screamed to be let out.

At the back of the room there was flapping, followed by the sound of feet landing on the carpet. She turned to the sound but could see only black. A warm trickle made its way down her legs.

She was sure she was still screaming but there was no response to confirm it.

She felt a cold breeze heading towards her. Her back was against the door. Her eyes wide, searching, but she saw nothing.

It was upon her in an instant. She put her hands up to her neck, but strong talons prised them away. Whatever it was, it looked her directly in the eyes. The drumming in her ears became louder. The screaming stopped. She fainted.

There was a guttural gurgle, as its teeth tore at her throat, it opened her trachea, and that hiss was her final sound.

Sated, it left her to be disposed of like the others. It unfurled its wings and ascended the loft ladder, pulling it up behind.

Mr Brown, its alter ego, was practised at covering its tracks and playing the innocent with the police – if he needed to. They had done this several times before, and in a couple of months, they would move to another town, find a little country guest house, and bide their time.

When they knew the urge would come again.

# The City of Stories

My mother was a sayer. Her mother was too, and so it goes. Except when it doesn't. When the polisnazers[*] stop you. That's why we need to leave this place. It's too dangerous for us now. The rumours have started.

It began when I was three. My mother would close the bedroom curtains and find her stowed torch to search the room, before sitting me on her knee. I loved those rare times, where I could feel my mother's breath on my face and smell the jasmine that engulfed her.

My heart fluttered every time she introduced something new. My favourites were always the animals that would come alive at her behest, with their fluffy tails and shiny eyes and charming antics. The pictures danced in my head, as if they were still surviving, but of course they weren't. *The Regime* had seen to that.

Now my daughter is three, and I need to get her away from this awful place, where people like us can't stay alive. We are sayers too and we are outlawed by *The Regime* that instructs all, that, *'None can tell tales from the yesteryear, lest they be struck down for heresy.'*

I am told there is a city far away from here where people like us can go, where we're welcomed, revered even, for keeping the old tradition alive. A city on a hill, surrounded by walls, which are guarded day and night by brave

---

[*] **Author's Note:** Polisnazers is a made-up word to suggest an oppressive regime in a dystopian future. A mix of, police, Stasi, Nazi, and snitches!

souls that fought back and won. A city where lights shine in the darkness. I hear that people gather in the square to listen to the old stories, whilst sentinels stand, their guns pointing from the turrets. Its name is now *Storyburh,* and I need to get there, for my daughter's sake.

The night is a perilous time here; no streetlights anymore and polisnazers on every corner, waiting for the lawless to emerge. I have my pocket lantern and a sack full of saved food, some spare clothes, two blankets, and soap to wash in the River Avon, if we make it that far.

I am reminded of my mother as I look through the shutters that replaced our curtains after the siege. I didn't realise how courageous she was then. Defying *the Regime* that had taken over our cosy world of stories – chronicles handed down from one generation to the next after *The Regime's* first ordered burning.

She was one of the chosen few who were able to recall them and regale the people with such tales that would make them happy and keep them energised. But the oppressors changed all that.

I slip the blood-spattered photograph of my mother into my pocket and lift my daughter from her slumber. Her hair is mussed, and my heart is full.

'We have to go,' I mouth, not daring to say the words out loud.

She understands. She is a sayer, and we must survive.

## Like to Read More Work Like This?

Then sign up to our mailing list and download our free collection of short stories, *Magnetism*. Sign up now to receive this free e-book and also to find out about all of our new publications and offers.

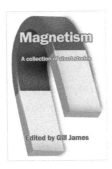

Sign up here:

http://eepurl.com/gbpdVz

## Please Leave a Review

Reviews are so important to writers. Please take the time to review this book. A couple of lines is fine.

Reviews help the book to become more visible to buyers. Retailers will promote books with multiple reviews.

This in turn helps us to sell more books... And then we can afford to publish more books like this one.

Leaving a review is very easy.
Go to https://smarturl.it/o8xz0u, scroll down the left-hand side of the Amazon page and click on the "Write a customer review" button.

# Other Publications by Chapeltown Books

## Ways of Seeing
## by Rick Vick

This collection of prose and poetry takes the reader on a journey through many aspects of life and indeed offers you many ways of seeing. It makes the reader take another look. Rick Vick's mantra was, "Let the pen do the writing." He had a love of people that manifested itself on every level, from the encouragement of a shy, new poet at one of his workshops to his record-breaking seven appearances as a writer at the prestigious Stroud Short Stories.

Sadly Rick died before we finished preparing this collection for publication. He has left us an inspiring legacy.

Order from Amazon:

ISBN: 978-1-910542-65-1 (paperback)
978-1-910542-66-8 (ebook)

**Chapeltown Books**

# Tripping the Flash Fantastic
## by Allison Symes

Allison Symes loves reading and writing quirky fiction. She discovered flash fiction thanks to a Cafélit challenge and has been hooked on the form ever since. In this follow-up to her *From Light to Dark and Back Again*, Allison will take you back in time, into some truly criminal minds, into fantasy worlds, and show you how motherhood looks from the viewpoint of a dragon. Enjoy the journey!

"Fabulous collection of poems and flash fiction. Some made me giggle, some made me gasp, all surprised me! Highly recommend this!" *(Amazon)*

Order from Amazon:

ISBN: 978-1-910542-58-3 (paperback)
978-1-910542-59-0 (ebook)

**Chapeltown Books**

# The World in an Eye
## by Maroula Blades

*The World In An Eye* is an eclectic collection. It ardently and boldly tackles issues that plague our societies. Presenting diverse flash fiction stories set in America, England, Germany, Italy and other places where poignancy, rawness and sensitivity are propelled to the foreground. This evocative compilation also thrusts taboo topics out from the fringes into the spotlight. Here, they explore and expose the lives of those not fed with golden spoons.

"A moving and haunting collection of short stories. Rich poetic words and thought provoking narrative. Take your own time and drink it in. Beautiful." *(Amazon)*

Order from Amazon:

ISBN: 978-1-910542-56-9 (paperback)
978-1-910542-57-6 (ebook)

**Chapeltown Books**

# Aftermath: Creative Responses to the 2020 Pandemic
## edited by Gill James

A continuing response by writers to the Covid19 pandemic in 2020 and during the ongoing aftershocks in 2021, this collection is of work by writers we have published before and whom we trust, and their trusted colleagues. When disasters strike writers respond and react in words. They share with us their hopes and fears. They describe and rationalise. Like its companion book, this volume contains pieces of fiction, flash fiction, script, poetry, memoir and some texts which cannot easily be categorised.

Order from Amazon:

ISBN: 978-1-910542-74-3 (paperback)
978-1-910542-75-0 (ebook)

**Chapeltown Books**